Gibbus Moony
Wants to Bite You!

Leslie Muir

Illustrated by Jen Corace

Atheneum Books for Young Readers

New York   London   Toronto   Sydney

ATHENEUM BOOKS FOR YOUNG READERS
An imprint of Simon & Schuster Children's Publishing Division
1230 Avenue of the Americas, New York, New York 10020
Text copyright © 2011 by Leslie Muir
Illustrations copyright © 2011 by Jen Corace
ATHENEUM BOOKS FOR YOUNG READERS is a registered trademark of
Simon & Schuster, Inc.
For information about special discounts for bulk purchases,
please contact Simon & Schuster Special Sales at 1-866-506-1949
or business@simonandschuster.com.
The Simon & Schuster Speakers Bureau can bring authors to your
live event. For more information or to book an event, contact the
Simon & Schuster Speakers Bureau at 1-866-248-3049 or visit our
website at www.simonspeakers.com.
Book design by Debra Sfetsios-Conover
The text for this book is set in Blue Century.
The illustrations for this book are rendered in pen, ink with
watercolor, and acrylic on paper.
Manufactured in the United States of America
0611 PCR
10 9 8 7 6 5 4 3 2
Library of Congress Cataloging-in-Publication Data
Muir, Leslie.
Gibbus Moony wants to bite you! / Leslie Muir ; illustrated by Jen
Corace. — 1st ed.
p. cm.
Summary: A young bat is eager to sink his newly emerging adult
fangs into a neck, although his parents and grandfather remind
him that they only bite fruit.
ISBN 978-1-4169-7905-0 (hardcover)
[1. Growth—Fiction. 2. Bats—Fiction. 3. Vampires—Fiction.]
I. Corace, Jen, ill. II. Title.
PZ7.M8838Gib 2011
[E]—dc22   2010009786

For Mom and Dad,
with love and boundless gratitude
—L. M.

To Miles
—J. C.

Gibbus Moony's baby fangs had _fallen_ out.

He **smiled** in the mirror. The teeny, tiny **tips** of his grown-up fangs t**wink**led.

No one could call Gibb the *baby*
of the family anymore.
  "Son, you're growing up," said Dad.
  "Soon you'll be a big vampire,"
said Mom.

"I *am* a big vampire," said Gibb. "**And I want to *bite* something.**"

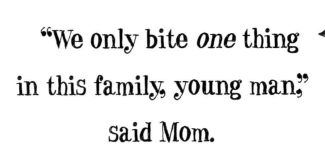

"We only bite *one* thing
in this family, young man,"
said Mom.

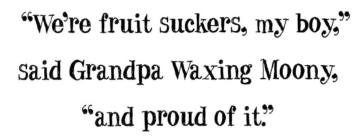

"We're fruit suckers, my boy,"
said Grandpa Waxing Moony,
"and proud of it."

"And that makes you a **nectarian**," said Dad.
"Not to be confused with those *other* vampire relatives."

"*Neck?* Neck! I'm a *necktarian!*"
Gibb felt *fangtabulous*.

"Now run along and
go swing from the rafters,"
suggested Mom.

But swinging was for sissies.

So Gibb snuck off to find something *juicy*.

He pounced on Werner, his stuffed gargoyle.

"Stop chewing your toys, Gibb. Werner's getting soggy."

Mom stuffed Werner in the washing machine.

He chomped on the family photo album.

"Quit that, Gibb.

You'll dent Uncle Orlok," said Dad.

He gnawed the neck
of the Stradivarius.
The strings popped.

Sweet success!

But Gibb wasn't satisfied.
He needed something big.
Something that moved.
Something that . . .

noticed.

So Gibbus Moony crept off
in search of the perfect bite.
He spied Grandpa
Waxing Moony, taking
his afternoon nap.

"**Beware!**" he whispered. "I'm Gibbus Moony, and I'm going to bite you!" He nibbled Grandpa's ear.

Grandpa giggled in his sleep.
"**Oooo** . . . that tickles."

"What do snoring grandpas know," grumbled Gibb.

He spied the gardener
trimming the topiaries.
Gibb flapped his cape.

"Prepare!"
he squealed.
"I'm Gibbus Moony,
and I'm going
to **bite** you!"

The gardener waved him away.
"Scram, mosquito."

"What do grumpy gardeners know," mumbled Gibb.

Gibb kicked a dandelion. How could he be a big vampire when his bite had no bite? He plopped under his favorite thinking tree next door.

Fall leaves rustled a sleepy lullaby. Gibb yawned.
Being a *necktarian* was **exhausting.**

Before long, he was dreaming. . . .

"OUCH!" Gibb's eyes popped open.

Something was pecking his nose.

The Something slobbered.

The Something had three teeth.

A porch door slammed.
"Watch out!" warned a boy.

Gibb escaped up his thinking tree.

"That's Mandy, my baby sister. We call her Mandibles. She bites everything—even rocks," said the boy.

Gibb flipped over

a branch and

**hung
upside
down.**

He peered down at the boy.

Could it be? The perfect bite?

Gibb licked his teeny fangs. "Come closer," he whispered.

"Well, I better
take care of *her* first."
The boy pulled
a bag of candy from
his pocket.

He tossed it in the air.

GUMMY BITES

"Fetch!"

Mandibles toddled after it.

"Coast is clear!" said the boy. He climbed up and
hung near Gibb. "This is my favorite branch too."
Gibb scooted closer. "Beware," he whispered.
"I'm Moe," said the boy. "We just moved in."

Gibb spread his cape.

"I'm Gibbus Moony, and I'm **going to bite** —"

"Biting's for babies," said Moe.

Babies?

"*Slobbery, stinky, diaper* babies,"
said Moe. "Like *her.*"

Gibb snapped his cape shut.
He wobbled.

"What are you doing down there?" asked Moe.

"Oh, uh . . . just looking for one of these." He handed an apple up to Moe.

Moe crunched. "Mmmmm. Upside-down apples are totally **toothsome**."

"Totally what?" asked Gibb.

"Toothsome. It means *dee*licious," said Moe.

Gibb bit his apple. It did taste especially toothsome.

Gibbus Moony and his
new friend hung out until
the crickets chirped.

"How about baseball tomorrow?"

"Sure," said Gibb. "I'll bring the bat."

Gibb skipped home in the shadows.

"How was your twilight?" asked Mom at dinner.
"Fangtastic," he said.

"Oh dear. Maybe it's time we had the Biting Talk," said Dad.

"Why? Biting is baby stuff," said Gibb, "I'm a big vampire now."

"Spoken like a true-blue Moony," said Grandpa.
"Now pass the blood-orange juice, my boy."

"What's for dessert?" asked Gibb.

Mom winked. "How does a big slice of pineapple upside-down cake sound?"

Gibb's grin spread to his pointy ears. "Totally **toothsome.**"

And it was.